GOODNIGHT

TiNY

MOUSE

an itty bitty bedtime story by

Heidi Anderson

TATE PUBLISHING & *Enterprises*

Published by Tate Publishing & Enterprises, LLC
127 E. Trade Center Terrace | Mustang, Oklahoma 73064 USA
1.888.361.9473 | www.tatepublishing.com

Tate Publishing is committed to excellence in the publishing industry. The company reflects the philosophy established by the founders, based on Psalm 68:11,
"The Lord gave the word and great was the company of those who published it."

Book design copyright © 2009 by Tate Publishing, LLC. All rights reserved.
Cover and Interior design by Elizabeth A. Mason
Illustrations by Benton Rudd

Published in the United States of America

ISBN: 978-1-60696-933-5
1. Juvenile Fiction: Bedtime & Dreams
2. Juvenile Fiction: Animals/Mice, Hamsters, Guinea Pigs
09.02.11

TO HERB, BRIDGET, & GAVIN
I LOVE YOU
ALWAYS AND FOREVER

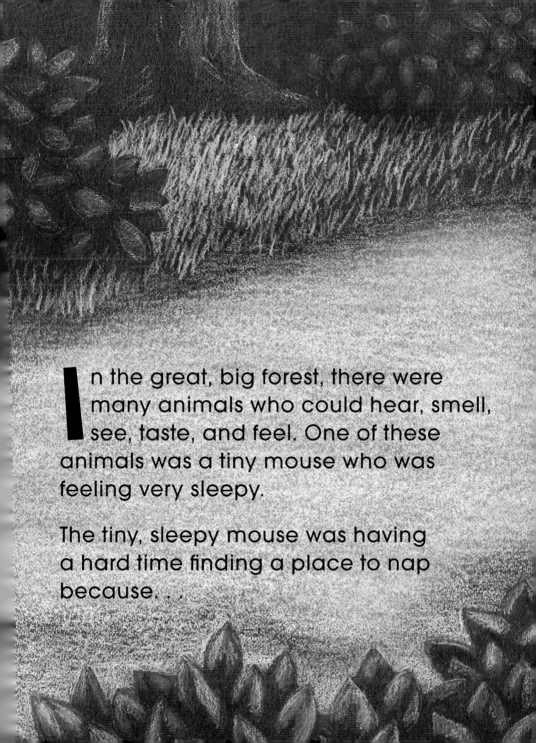

In the great, big forest, there were many animals who could hear, smell, see, taste, and feel. One of these animals was a tiny mouse who was feeling very sleepy.

The tiny, sleepy mouse was having a hard time finding a place to nap because. . .

There was the DEER who could hear
the tiny mouse.

There was the **BEAR** who could smell the tiny mouse.

There was the **EAGLE** who could see the tiny mouse.

There was the TROUT who could taste the tiny mouse.

There was even a little GIRL
who could *feel* the tiny mouse

RUNNING RIGHT UP HER LEG!

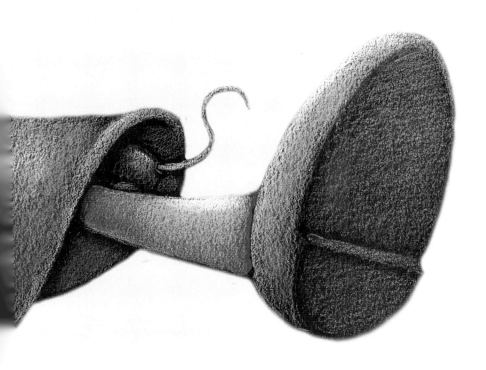

"Oh!" the little girl cried, "Tiny mouse, tiny mouse please go away!"

"But I'm so sleepy," yawned the tiny mouse, "and your leg looked like such a good place to nap."

"Instead of running up my leg, go run up the deer's leg!" cried the little girl.

"But the deer can hear me coming," squeaked the tiny mouse.

"Well," said the little girl, "go run up the bear's leg!"

"But the bear can smell me coming," squeaked the tiny mouse.

"Well," said the little girl, "go run up the eagle's leg!"

"But the eagle can see me coming," squeaked the tiny mouse.

"Let me guess," said the little girl. "You will not run up the trout's leg because it can taste you coming?"

"No, silly girl," laughed the tiny mouse. "I can't run up a trout's leg. . .

Fish have no Legs!"

The little girl had an idea to help the tiny, sleepy mouse. She looked all around and found a tiny hole for the tiny mouse to take a nap.

"I found a tiny hole just right for a tiny mouse," she said.

"There the deer will not hear you, the bear will not smell you, the eagle will not see you, the trout will not taste you, and I don't have to feel you running right up my leg!"

"Oh, thank you so much for helping! You have found me a place to nap away from the many animals of the great, big forest," squeaked the tiny mouse.

"Goodnight tiny mouse," said the little girl.

"Goodnight little girl," the tiny mouse squeaked.

With a great, big yawn, the tiny mouse ran down the tiny hole and took a tiny nap.

listen|imagine|view|experience